W9-AJR-209

For all the Nickerson kids: Lucy, Zach, Emmy, Ella, Benji, and Ian

Text Copyright and Illustration Copyright © 2019 Marty Kelley

Sleeping Bear Press®
2395 South Huron Parkway, Suite 200
Ann Arbor, MI 48104
www.sleepingbearpress.com

Printed and bound in the United States.

10 9 8 7 6 5 4 3 2 1

Library of Congress Cataloging-in-Publication Data

Names: Kelley, Marty, author, illustrator.
Title: Experiment #256 / written and illustrated by Marty Kelley.
Other titles: Experiment number 256 | Experiment number two hundred fifty-six
Description: Ann Arbor, MI : Sleeping Bear Press, [2019] | Summary: In his
science journal, Ian records that his experiments with a jet pack for his
dog, Wilbur, lead to chaos and a lot of unhappy people.
Identifiers: LCCN 2019009905 | ISBN 9781534110137 (hardcover)
Subjects: | CYAC: Science—Experiments—Fiction. | Inventions—Fiction. |
Dogs—Fiction. | Humorous stories.
Classification: LCC PZ7.K28172 Exp 2019 | DDC [E]—dc23
LC record available at https://lccn.loc.gov/2019009905

Experiment #256

By
Marty
Kelley

NOTES
• Garden fence needs some repairs.
• Wilbur got tangled up in the undies that Mrs. Marino was hanging on the line.
• Mrs. Marino is not happy.

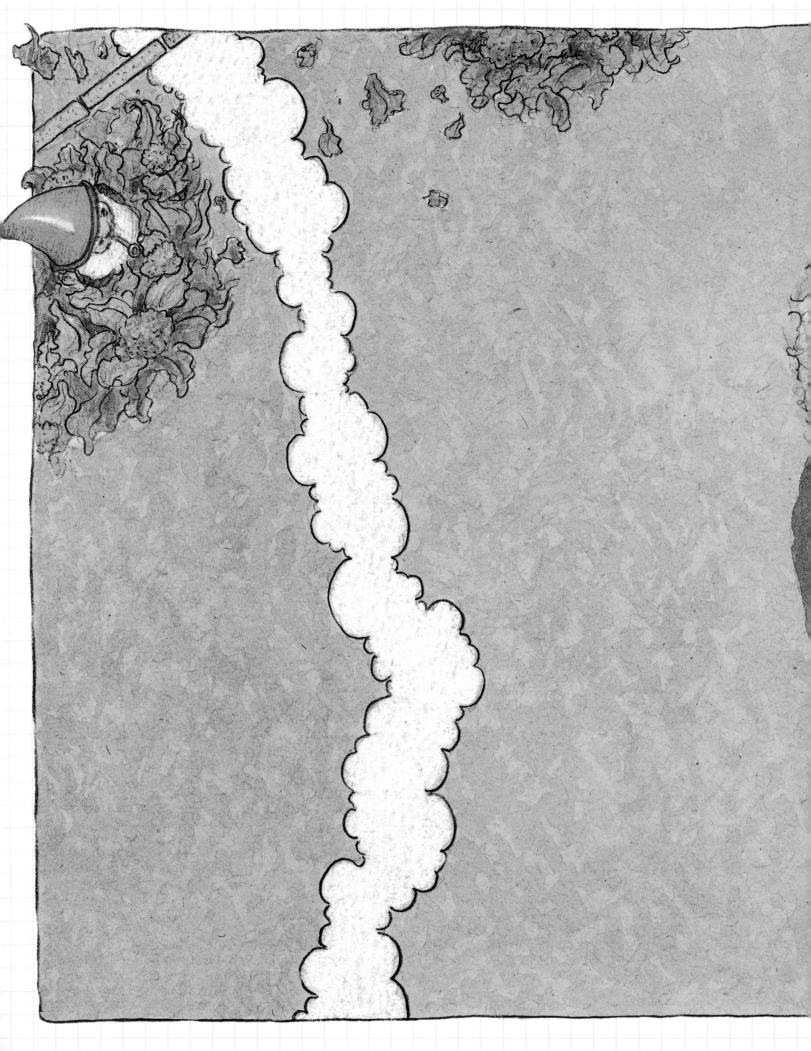

NOTES
• Straps on jet pack not secure.
• Wilbur brought Mrs. Marino's undies back.
• Mrs. Marino is STILL not happy.

CONCLUSION
Building a jet pack for my dog was not the best idea I have ever had.

NOTES
• Wilbur is not happy.

5